Ashley Small & Ashlee Tall

BEST FRIENDS FOREVER?

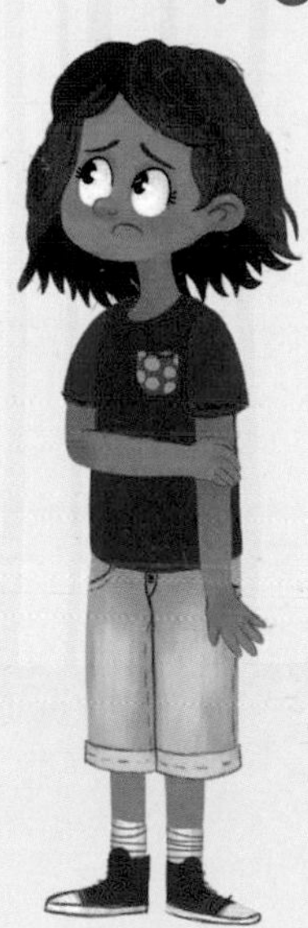

by Michele Jakubowski

Illustrated by Hédi Fekete

Raintree is an imprint of Capstone Global Library Limited, a company incorporated in England and Wales having its registered office at 264 Banbury Road, Oxford, OX2 7DY – Registered company number: 6695582

www.raintree.co.uk
myorders@raintree.co.uk

Edited by Eliza Leahy and Helen Cox Cannons
Designed by Lori Bye
Original illustrations © Capstone 2016
Illustrated by Hédi Fekete
Production by Laura Manthe
Printed and bound in China

ISBN 978 1 4747 2040 3
20 19 18 17 16
10 9 8 7 6 5 4 3 2 1

British Library Cataloguing in Publication Data
A full catalogue record for this book is available from the British Library.

Acknowledgements
Every effort has been made to contact copyright holders of material reproduced in this book. Any omissions will be rectified in subsequent printings if notice is given to the publisher.

contents

Ashley "Ash" Sanchez may be small, but she's mighty! Ash likes to play all types of games – from sport to video games – and she loves to win. Ash may be loud and silly, but more than anything, she is a great friend!

Ashlee Taylor, otherwise known as Lee, is tall and graceful. When Lee is not twirling around at her dance classes, she can be found drawing or painting. Lee may be shy around new people, but she is very kind!

chapter one

RAINY DAY

It was a very rainy day – too wet to go outside and play. Best friends Ashley Sanchez and Ashlee Taylor were stuck inside the Sanchezes' apartment with nothing to do.

"We could build a fort," Ashley said.

"I don't feel like doing that," replied Ashlee.

Even though they shared a name, and were both eight years old, Ashlee and Ashley were different in almost every way.

Ashlee Taylor's friends liked to call her Lee. She was tall and a bit shy. Ashley Sanchez was known as Ash. She was small and outgoing.

Lee and Ash were always together. Their friends started calling them Ashley Small and Ashlee Tall.

"I've got an idea!" Ash said.

She jumped off the sofa and bounced out of the room. When she returned, she was carrying a huge book.

Lee knew straight away what it was. "Your photo album!" she cheered. "Let me go and get mine."

Lee jumped up gracefully. She skipped out of the apartment. When she returned a few minutes later, she was carrying her own photo album.

The girls settled down beside each other on the sofa. They opened their books.

"Here I am as a baby," Ash said. She pointed at the first picture in her book.

Ash had been born in winter. In the picture she was bundled up in a coat. Her mum was standing on the steps of their apartment building and holding her.

"Here's my baby picture," Lee said. She pointed at a photo in her book.

Lee had been born in summer. In her picture she wore a sundress with tiny flowers on it. Her mum was holding her in front of the very same apartment building.

Ash and Lee had been born exactly six months apart. They had both been brought home to the same apartment building. They had lived opposite from each other on the same floor ever since.

Ash and Lee flipped through their albums together.

Ash's album was messy. It was filled with pictures of her playing basketball and other sports. There were also pictures of her baby brother, Sam, when he was just born. The pictures didn't all fit in the book, and some fell out onto the sofa as she turned the pages.

Lee's book was neat and tidy. With her mum's help, she had labelled everything. She had lots of pictures from her dance recitals. There were also old pieces of her artwork.

"Here we are on our very first day of kindergarten," Ash said. "We were so little!"

First day of school

Lee looked over at the picture. In it, the two of them were standing in front of a school bus. Even then Lee was almost twice as tall as Ash. "Well, *you* were little," Lee said.

Ash laughed. "Look at this one!" She pointed to a picture from when they were both babies. They were eating spaghetti and making a huge mess.

"Look at all that sauce on my face," said Ash. "I still eat spaghetti like that!"

Lee looked more closely at the picture. She asked, "Is that pasta coming out of my nose? Gross!"

They laughed and giggled as they shared their albums. The time passed quickly. Before they knew it, Lee had to go home for dinner.

"See you later," Lee said. She went to her apartment.

"Have a good dinner," Ash called. "I hope no spaghetti comes out of your nose!"

chapter two

BIG NEWS

"Do you know what my favourite ice-cream flavour is?" asked Lee.

Ash knew that Lee's absolute favourite was chocolate. She loved anything with chocolate!

Just to be silly, she replied, "Vanilla?"

Lee looked at her friend to see if she was serious.

Ash started laughing. "Just kidding! I know it's chocolate!"

"I can't believe you don't like ice cream," Lee said.

"It's okay," Ash said. "Anyway, you like it enough for both of us."

Lee was staying at Ash's apartment for the day. Lee's parents were out doing errands, and they had been gone for a long time. That was okay with Lee and Ash. It meant they had more time to play together. They were tidying up their mess of clothes, books and games when they heard Lee's parents return.

The girls knew they could keep playing. Mrs Taylor and Mrs Sanchez would talk for a long time. Just like Ash and Lee, their mums were also best friends.

The girls were taking out a board game when they heard Ash's mum shout, "That's wonderful!"

Both Ash and Lee wanted to know what was so wonderful. They jumped up to go and find out.

In the living room, their mums were hugging. Mrs Sanchez said, "I'm so happy for you!"

"What's everybody so excited about?" asked Lee.

Mrs Taylor looked at Mr Taylor. Then she turned to Lee and said, "We were going to wait for your sister, but I suppose we can tell you now."

Lee's older sister, Mallory, was spending the day with her friend Jade.

"Tell me what?" asked Lee.

Mr and Mrs Taylor smiled at each other. Then Mr Taylor said, "We're moving, Lee! We found a nice house just three streets from here. You are going to love it!"

Lee was confused. Her parents had talked about moving before. They said it could take a while to find a house. It had been so long since they'd mentioned it that Lee had forgotten all about it.

"I am?" Lee asked.

"Oh, yes!" Mrs Taylor said. "There is a back garden to play in. And you'll have your own room!"

Lee had been sharing a bedroom with Mallory her entire life. She liked the idea of having her own room.

Lee turned towards Ash. "My own room! Isn't that great?"

"Um, sure," replied Ash. But she wasn't sure at all.

chapter three

{ CHANGES }

A few days later, Ash was still not sure. Her best friend was moving, and she didn't know how she felt about that. She sat at the kitchen table. Her head rested on her fists. There was a grumpy frown on her face.

"What's wrong, Bunny?" her mum asked.

Usually Ash didn't like it when her mum called her "Bunny". Today she was too grumpy to argue.

"Why does Lee have to move?" Ash pouted.

Mrs Sanchez had been feeding Ash's baby brother, Sam. She put down the spoon. "The Taylors want to live somewhere bigger," she said.

Sam didn't like that his mum had stopped feeding him. He stretched out his arms and legs and waved his hands. Ash thought he looked silly, but she was too grumpy to giggle.

"Their apartment is big enough," Ash argued.

"It will be nice for Lee to have her own room," Mrs Sanchez said.

The Taylors' apartment was very similar to the Sanchezes'. Both had three bedrooms. Mr Taylor worked at home. He used one of the bedrooms for an office. Lee and Mallory shared the other room.

"I suppose," Ash said. She did like having her own room. But she also liked having Lee living opposite them.

Mrs Sanchez put down the spoon again. She said, "I've got an idea! Why don't you see if Lee can sleep over tonight? They've been so busy packing. It might be nice for her to take a break."

Sam stretched out his arms and legs again. This time his face got very red. He looked funny. Ash was feeling better, so she laughed.

"That's a great idea," she told her mum. "I'm going to ask her right now."

Mrs Sanchez put a spoonful of food into Sam's mouth. Ash turned and marched happily out of the room.

Ash swung open her front door. At that very moment, Lee was walking out of her apartment opposite. She was carrying a big purple duffle bag.

"Fancy meeting you here!" Ash said.

"Yes, indeed!" Lee replied.

"Guess what? My mum said you could sleep over tonight!" Ash said.

Lee frowned. "I can't. Madeline from dance asked me to sleep over after class tonight."

Ash frowned too. She said, “But you never sleep over at other people’s houses.”

It was true. Ash loved to have sleepovers with other friends. But Lee had only ever slept over at Ash’s. Lee had been asked by others, but she’d always said no. She worried she would miss her mum and dad too much.

“I know,” Lee said. “I think I’m ready to try.”

“Oh,” Ash said sadly.

“You’d really like Madeline. Maybe we can all play one day?” Lee said.

The door opened, and Mr Taylor walked out. "Hi, Ash!" he said. Then he turned to Lee. "Ready to go?"

"Yep!" Lee said. "See you later, Ash!"

"Bye," Ash said. Then she went straight back to being grumpy.

chapter four

THE FIGHT

Lee had so much fun sleeping over at Madeline's house. She had stayed the whole night without wanting to go home!

Her parents picked her up the next morning. They drove past her new house on the way home. Her mum pointed to the window of what would be Lee's room. She couldn't wait to live there!

Before they could move, though, Lee had to pack up her stuff. It was a boring job. Lee and her mum were in her room, deciding what she should keep and what to get rid of.

"What about this one?" Mrs Taylor asked. She picked a pink T-shirt out of a pile of clothes in Lee's wardrobe and held it up. It had the words "Just Dance" on the front. It was one of Lee's favourites.

Lee noticed a small chocolate stain on the front. "Put it in the pile for charity," she told her mum. She didn't like it when her clothes were messy.

Almost everything from Lee's wardrobe had been cleared out. She went inside to take out the last few items.

In the very back of the wardrobe, she found a shoebox. There was writing on the lid. It read, "Ash & Lee Time Capsule".

"Our time capsule!" Lee cheered.

"What is that?" Mrs Taylor asked.

"Ash and I learned about them at school two years ago," Lee said. "You put things in a box. Then you hide it somewhere and wait a long time to open it. It helps you remember things later that are special today."

Lee opened the box. Inside were stickers and drawings. There was a wrapper from Lee's favourite chocolate bar. There was also an award Ash had won playing basketball. At the bottom was a picture of Lee and Ash.

Lee showed her mum the picture. "It's from our first sleepover," she said.

Suddenly, Lee felt sad. She was going to miss living opposite from Ash. She knew things wouldn't be the same.

Mrs Taylor gave Lee a hug. "Why don't we take a break?" she said. "Maybe you can see if Ash can play."

Lee hopped up and twirled out of her room. Playing with her best friend was just what she needed!

* * *

When Ash opened her door, she did not look happy to see Lee. She didn't like that everything was changing.

"Want to play?" asked Lee.

"You're not too busy with Madeline?" replied Ash in a grumpy voice. "I thought maybe she was your best friend now."

"No," Lee said softly. She didn't like the way Ash was talking to her. She also didn't like to fight.

"I've got basketball practice with my other friends soon. I can't play," Ash said. "Maybe I'll see you around."

Lee felt like she was going to cry. She quickly said goodbye. Then she rushed back to her apartment.

Ash slammed her door shut. She went from feeling mad to sad. Tears streamed down her cheeks. Why did everything have to change?

chapter five

NOT ALL BAD

Mrs Sanchez heard Ash crying. She came into the room to see what was wrong.

"Oh, Ash! What's the matter?" Mrs Sanchez asked.

"I don't have a best friend anymore," Ash said. Saying it out loud made her cry harder.

Mrs Sanchez was confused. She asked, "What do you mean?"

Ash explained. "I was rude to Lee. Now she's moving away. What if she doesn't want to be my best friend anymore?"

Mrs Sanchez put her arm around Ash. She said, "You and Lee have been friends for a long time. I don't think one fight is going to end that."

Ash still felt sad. "Everything is going to be different," she said.

Mrs Sanchez nodded. "It will be different," she said. "But it's not all bad."

Ash sat up and looked at her mum. "Yes it is! My best friend is moving away!"

Mrs Sanchez said, "Don't forget, my best friend is moving away too."

Ash hadn't thought of that. "Then how can you say it's not all bad?"

"I'm trying to think about the good things," Mrs Sanchez said. "I'm glad that they aren't moving very far away. We'll still be able to see them a lot."

"That's true," Ash said.

"Most of all, I'm happy that my friend is happy," Mrs Sanchez said. "I know they have wanted a bigger home for a long time. I'm happy they found one close by!"

Ash remembered how happy Lee had been about her new bedroom. "I suppose so," she said, flopping onto the sofa.

"The friendship you have with Lee is very special," Mrs Sanchez said. "Nothing will change that. Best friends are always best friends, no matter how far apart they live."

It helped Ash to know that her mum was going to miss her best friend too. She started to feel a bit better. But then Ash remembered how she had treated Lee.

"I wasn't very nice to Lee," she said softly. "What if she moves and forgets all about me?"

Mrs Sanchez spotted the photo album sitting on the coffee table. She smiled and said, "I've got a great idea!"

chapter six

BACK TO NORMAL

Lee and her family had been living in their new house for three days. Moving had been hard work, but it was also a lot of fun.

Lee loved her new room! Her mum and dad had let her help decorate. They had painted the room her favourite shade of purple.

Lee had picked out a shaggy purple rug with lavender polka dots for the floor. She had a new white desk. It fitted perfectly under the window that faced the street.

The Sanchez family was coming over for dinner that night. Lee was nervous. Ash had been away visiting her grandparents. Lee hadn't seen her since their fight.

"Knock, knock," Mrs Taylor said as she walked into Lee's room. Her arms were full of folded laundry. She noticed that Lee looked sad. "What's wrong?" she asked.

Lee frowned and said, "Will things be different with Ash and me now? What if she doesn't want to be my friend anymore?"

Mrs Taylor sat on the bed. She said, "Things will be different. It will take us a while to get used to, but we will. You and Ash are too close to let this end your friendship."

Lee didn't look so sure.

"I've got an idea," her mum said. "We've got a little time before they get here. Where are your art supplies?"

* * *

A couple of hours later, the Sanchez family arrived at Lee's new house.

"Your new house is cool," Ash mumbled.

"Thanks," Lee said softly.

Both of them wanted things to feel normal, but they didn't.

"Lee, why don't you show Ash your new room?" Mrs Taylor said.

"Good idea," Mrs Sanchez said. She whispered to Ash, "Don't forget what you brought."

They walked into Lee's new room. Lee noticed that Ash was carrying something.

"I, uh, just wanted to say I'm sorry," Ash said.

"Thanks," said Lee. "I'm sorry too."

Ash unrolled her poster board. Across the top she had written their names and "best friends forever!" Below she had drawn a picture of the two of them.

In the spaces she had stuck on cut-out pictures of Lee's favourite things. There were dance shoes, paintbrushes and chocolate desserts. She had also stuck on some pictures of the two of them. She decorated the background with hearts and stars.

Ash pointed to one of the pictures. "When we were looking at our photo albums, you said this was your favourite picture," she said.

It was a picture of them together after one of Lee's many dance recitals. Lee had been so happy that Ash had come to see her dance.

"It is," Lee said. "Thank you so much!"

Lee knelt down. She pulled something out from under her bed and held it out to Ash. "I made this for you."

It was a piece of poster board like the one Ash had used. Lee had drawn a fancy border around the edges. In the middle she had written "Ashlee & Ashley" and below that, "best friends forever".

She had drawn some of Ash's favourite things. There was a basketball, pizza and musical notes. In the centre, there was a picture of Ash teaching Lee how to hit a softball.

"I remember that day," Ash said. She pointed to the picture. "It took you all day, but you finally hit the softball!"

Lee nodded and smiled. "Remember when I fell down from swinging too hard?" she asked.

The friends laughed. When they stopped, they heard their mums laughing together downstairs.

"The best friend board was my mum's idea," Ash said.

"Mine too!" Lee replied. "Our mums are such good friends, they even think alike!"

Ash smiled. "Do you think we'll be best friends when we're as old as they are?" she asked.

Lee smiled back. "Yes. We'll be best friends forever!"

GLOSSARY

bundled wrapped or gathered together

confused uncertain about something

decorate add colour, design or other features that improve the look of something

excited eager and interested

gracefully smoothly

grumpy sulky or easily annoyed

lavender a pale bluish-purple colour

recitals performances, usually given by one performer or a small group

shaggy having or covered with long, rough hair or wool

time capsule container that holds objects from the present time and is meant to be opened by someone in the future in order to see what life was like in the past

TALK ABOUT IT

1. When Lee's parents announce that the family is moving, Lee and Ash have different responses. Talk about some possible reasons why they had such different feelings about the move.

2. Do you think the two girls will stay best friends, even now that they're not living opposite from one another? Discuss why or why not.

3. Pick one of the two main characters, Ash or Lee, and discuss why you would or would not like to have her as a friend.

WRITE IT DOWN

1. How do Ash and Lee show that they are good friends to one another? Write a poem about a time when you've been a good friend.

2. What are some things that are good about the Taylor family's move? What are some bad things about it? Make a list of pros and cons using examples from the text.

3. Ash and Lee are very different from one another, but they are best friends. Using examples from the text, name five ways that the two girls are different. Then write a paragraph about someone you care about who is very different from you.

MAKE YOUR OWN BEST FRIEND BOARD

Lee and Ash each make a surprise gift for one another after they get into an argument. Make your own best friend board using your creativity and some easy-to-find supplies!

what you need

- poster board
- felt-tips, crayons or coloured pencils
- glue
- photos
- magazines (for finding pictures and words to cut out)
- scissors

Whatever else you can think of that represents your friend or your friendship with one another: tickets from a film you saw together, cut-out pictures of your friend's favourite activities and words that describe your friend are just a few ideas!

what you do

Write your friend's name at the top of your poster board followed by a plus sign and your own name. Then write: Best Friends Forever!

Find some old magazines and flick through them to find pictures and words that represent your friend and the things that he or she likes to do. Cut them out and glue them onto your poster board. If you have photos of your friend, you could use those too.

Add designs and colour to your poster board. Draw borders and patterns. Draw more things that represent your BFF, if you like. Add anything else you think will help to make it shine! Glitter, ribbons, string and pipe cleaners are all good options.

ABOUT THE AUTHOR

Michele Jakubowski has the teachers in her life to thank for her love of reading and writing. While writing has always been a passion for Michele, she believes it is the books she has read throughout the years, and the teachers who recommended them, that have made her the storyteller she is today. Michele lives in Ohio, USA, with her husband, John, and their children, Jack and Mia.

ABOUT THE ILLUSTRATOR

Born in Transylvania, Hédi Fekete grew up watching and drawing her favourite cartoon characters. Each night, her mother read her beautiful bedtime stories, which made her love for storytelling grow. Hédi's love for books and animation stuck with her through the years, inspiring her to become an illustrator, digital artist and animator.

MAKE SURE TO CHECK OUT ALL THE TITLES IN THE ASHLEY SMALL AND ASHLEE TALL SERIES!

BEST FRIENDS FOREVER?

BRUSHES AND BASKETBALLS

THE GRASS IS ALWAYS GREENER

THE SLEEPOVER